# Why the Turtle and the Snail Carried their houses on Their Backs

To: Finn on his
Second birthday

Marilyn Laing
November 29th, 2023

Marilyn Laing

Printed in the United States of America.

Library of Congress Control Number: 2011901990

| ISBN | Paperback | 978-1-68536-455-7 |
| --- | --- | --- |
| | eBook | 978-1-68536-456-4 |

**Westwood Books Publishing LLC**
Atlanta Financial Center
3343 Peachtree Rd NE Ste 145-725
Atlanta, GA 30326

www.westwoodbookspublishing.com

# Introduction

Tiny the Turtle and Shelly Snail had been friends since preschool. They loved to play in the open forest that was near their home. They constantly ran along the cool stream pretending to be in their personal swimming pools. Tiny would always dream of the day when he would entertain friends and family in his very own home. They both knew what type of house that would suit each of them. Tiny needed and indoor swimming pool and a sand box, while Shelly needed cool rocks and large indoor-outdoor plants to compliment her dwelling.

With this in mind, the two set out to find their unique houses.

RESTAURANT
GOOD
FOOD

First, they passed by a beautiful building with lots of people inside. The aroma of freshly, cooked food floated through each window and door. Tiny was speechless as they stared at the building and their mouths watered. After a while, Tiny found his voice as he approached the patron. “Excuse me,” he said, “we would like to purchase this building for our home; it’s lovely indeed.”

“Oh no,” said the lovely patron dressed in crisp uniform, “this is no place to live, this is a restaurant. People come here for meals when they want to avoid cooking or just relax as they eat spending time with family and friends. You will have to look somewhere else for a home.”

HOTEL
FEEL GOOD
TAXI

Tiny and Shelly continued walking. There were lots of tall buildings in the area. Soon they came across a building with lots of beautiful windows. There were also sliding glass doors from each floor top to bottom. Inside a glass door moved from one floor to another transporting guests and their luggage. This door was called an elevator. Phones rang and people were busy dragging carts filled with luggage in and outside the building.

“Pardon me,” said Shelly, is this a good place to call home?”

“I don’t think so, replied the Bellman who was stationed at the door. Here tourist and business men and women spend money to live temporarily while they are away from their homes. This is called a hotel.” said the Bellman. “Besides, this is much too large for a small snail like yourself. Good luck as you search for your home.”

LASTING MEMORIAL HOSPITAL

Tiny and Shelly were such slow animals and their short legs were getting tired. They stopped at the Lasting Memorial Hospital. There they saw people in wheel chairs and on crutches. Babies were crying and mothers desperately tried to comfort them. The two decided this was not the home they were looking for.

GAS
$1.00

Later, they passed by a pumping station. Cars lined the tar mat near fuel pumps waiting for petrol. Attendants ran back and forth to allow the busy crowd to move quickly. The air was filled with smelly fumes so Shelly and Tiny hastened to move away from the station.

CITY BANK
LOANS
CASH

At the bank, customers waited on long lines inside and at the drive through for cashiers to complete their transactions. Bells and machines could be heard none stop. No one paid any attention to the two small creatures that were slowly moving about. After a few minutes the two left the way they came.

COMMERCIAL
CENTER

Near the bank was a large building that was the headquarters for the town's business. Residents also visited this site to publish documents for land and buildings locally. Hundreds of steps lined the building in and out. Just the thought of climbing up and down the steps each day made the two friends continued their search for a special home.

Tiny and Shelly were now exhausted from the long walk. Suddenly, they saw a delightful park. Water was climbing high in the air. The two friends could hardly believe their eyes. They crawled over the soft grass and dipped their tired feet in the cool water. They also got a long drink from the pond before moving along.

They had not gone far when they saw an ant named Andy. Where can we find a nice house to live in?" they asked. We have been looking for days and still have not found any houses to our liking. "You must check the places called residential," said Andy.

After thanking Andy, Shelly and Tiny took the bus to East End, West End, Pioneer's Point and Miles Stone. They crawled around many other small towns but to no avail.

"There is no use," cried Shelly with frustration, "we will grow old and never have the perfect house to call our own."

Suddenly, Tiny got a great idea. There on the side of a grassy path lay the most beautiful shells. The shells sparkled as the sun rays danced on them from the nearby ocean. “This is just what we have been looking for,” said Tiny with excitement, “A house that’s big enough to sleep in yet light enough to carry on our backs.” Let’s try them out, they shouted.

Slowly, the two crawled in their shells moving this way and that to get a feel of the surrounding space. Because they were so tired from days of walking, Shelly and Tiny fell fast asleep. And from that day the Turtle and the Snail carried their houses on their backs.

# Acknowledgements

Why the Turtle and The Snail Carried Their Houses on Their Backs is a Bahamian folklore. This book will help children to identify a variety of buildings in their communities and recognize how they are used.

Come enjoy the life of my new friends Shelly and Tiny as they search for their unique homes.

To: Ivan Reid for your wonderful illustrations. You saw those pictures through my eyes and made them beautiful.

To: Ronnie my husband. Thank you for encouraging me to take the big step and call a publisher. It was the best choice I could ever make.

## About the Author

The author is privileged to be a resident
of Grand Bahama Island, Bahamas.
After working in early childhood education
For over sixteen years, she decided to create
A platform to experience the world through
the eyes of a children. Shelly and Tiny
Adventure series seeks to visit childlike
experiences and turn them into fun
and enjoyable reading for children.

Why the Turtle and the Snail carried
their houses on their Backs is the
first of many books to come.

Read and travel with me.

Email: shellyandtinyadventures@gmail.com

Coming Soon

Shelly's Big Surprise

Shelly goes to Preschool

Shelly meets Friends on Grand Bahama Island

Made in the USA
Middletown, DE
14 April 2022